THE HOBBIT™

THE DESOLATION OF SMAUG

VISUAL COMPANION

JUDE FISHER

HOUGHTON MIFFLIN HARCOURT

BOSTON NEW YORK

2013

CONTENTS

INTRODUCTION
BY RICHARD ARMITAGE

What a privilege it is to be asked to provide an introduction to Jude Fisher's Visual Companion to *The Hobbit: The Desolation of Smaug*. It is with great pride that I am able to share some of my thoughts and experiences from my time working on the movies, playing Thorin Oakenshield.

The Hobbit has been in my life since I was about 7 years old. It was one of the first books I managed to read from cover to cover, on my own. This was largely due to a great teacher I had at primary school – Mrs O'Leary – who was brilliant at doing all the voices of the characters. This is where I began my *Hobbit* journey. Then I played an elf in a stage production of *The Hobbit*, at the Alexandra Theatre in Birmingham, England. This was one of my first stage appearances, so as you can see, this story has been with me for quite some years.

When I was preparing for the role of Thorin, I spent time reading many of Tolkien's other works, hunting down anything which would help me to imagine what it might be like to live as this 'very important Dwarf' (Tolkien's words, not mine), and I listened to an old BBC radio recording of Tolkien reading his own works. *The Hobbit* was a gift to his own children, offered to them in bedtime instalments, which comes as no surprise, since it reads so well aloud.

For me, finding Thorin's voice was key to understanding and revealing him: a voice that could command an army, and at the same time grieve for the loss of his kingdom and hope for its reclamation. Physically, he had to be a fearless fighter, a brave warrior-prince who understood war, its glory and its price. He had seen such devastation as a young prince, when the dragon came to Erebor. He had seen his people killed, or at best exiled, the wealth of his kingdom stolen by Smaug. It was essential to try and bear these scars in my portrayal of Thorin.

The personal quest which Thorin embarks on is complex. He yearns for the Lonely Mountain, for it is the place of his birth and of his birthright. He knows of the extraordinary wealth which lies within, but he has also witnessed the horror which lies within, embodied in the dragon that now inhabits the mountain-halls. He is haunted by the madness of his grandfather Thrór, a sickness caused by the hoarded gold treasure. Would Thorin also be afflicted by a susceptibility to that illness? Would it keep him from entering through the secret door, or would it tempt him deeper inside?

At a time in our own history when the imbalance of wealth in this world is so great, and the quest for riches – fuelled by greed – has caused men to isolate themselves and divide the societies they claim to serve, it has been fascinating to portray a character mentally and physically corrupted by gold, whilst at the same time believing in his own rationale.

One only has to substitute 'oil' for 'gold' – or any commodity coveted in our modern world – to see that Thorin's desire to protect what he regards as rightfully his, and to return to his own people what once was stolen, lies less in the realm of fantasy and feels much closer to home.

THE
JOURNEY SO FAR

The Company of Thorin Oakenshield has come a long way since assembling at Bag End, Bilbo Baggins's very comfortable hobbit-hole in the Shire town of Hobbiton. With the purpose of journeying to the Lonely Mountain, they seek to take back the lost Dwarven homeland of Erebor from the fearsome dragon that currently occupies it.

After eating their host out of house and home, the Company rode out of the hobbit-lands of the Shire into the world beyond. As they passed through the dangerous Trollshaws they encountered three enormous trolls with a taste for hobbit and Dwarf-flesh. Thankfully, due to a combination of considerable ingenuity on Bilbo's part, lucky timing and the help of the wizard Gandalf they left them turned to stone.

Passing over the edge of the Wild, the Company were pursued by Orcs riding upon savage Wargs, and with the help of Radagast they managed to escape through the Hidden Pass to the sanctuary of the Last Homely House in the West in the valley of Rivendell. Here they were able to rest and eat among the Elves, while Gandalf met with the Lady Galadriel, Lord Elrond and the wizard Saruman the White to discuss the growing menace in the East.

Sneaking secretly away from Rivendell before the Elves could prevent them from continuing their quest, Bilbo and the Dwarves made their way on steep and perilous paths up into the Misty Mountains, barely surviving a battle between two Stone Giants, before falling into a trap set by Goblins.

There, in the Goblin kingdom beneath the Misty Mountains, Thorin and his Dwarves were taken captive by the Great Goblin, while Bilbo fell further down into the mountain and came upon an even more unnerving creature.

Gollum lives among the roots of the mountain, in a dark place full of water and echoing caverns. There, he feeds on unwary travellers and pale fish that have never seen the light of day. By means of a riddle contest and some trickery, Bilbo managed to escape and take with him a golden ring that Gollum refers to as his 'precious', thus proving his abilities as a burglar.

Rescued by Gandalf and their own wits and courage, the Company emerged from the Goblin realm, only to be attacked once more by Orcs led by Azog the Defiler on his huge white Warg. They climbed up into the trees to evade their pursuers, and would have succumbed to the tenacious Wargs and to fire had it not been for an exciting rescue by the giant Eagles. Flying them out of harm's way, the Eagles placed them on top of the Carrock, a great rock that stands above the River Anduin.

So ended the Company's adventures in the Misty Mountains. Now they must carry on towards the distant peak of the Lonely Mountain, and to the Desolation of Smaug.

THORIN OAKENSHIELD

The Company of Dwarves, along with their indentured burglar, Bilbo Baggins, are making their journey to the Lonely Mountain under the command of Thorin Oakenshield, the Dwarven King-in-Exile. As a symbol of his status, Thorin wears a ring of kingship which serves as a reminder to him – and to others – that one day he will claim his birthright as the King Under the Mountain.

As a young prince, Thorin witnessed the terrible death and destruction that Smaug the Dragon brought upon his people. These scenes of devastation have forged in him a powerful sense of purpose. He has vowed to destroy the monster and restore the kingdom to his people, a vow that has made him both obdurate and unbending as he pushes the Company on through ever-greater danger.

Already, he and his Company have survived many perils, and the journey has strengthened their bonds. Each has proved his worth along the way, especially Bilbo, who has taken many steps towards proving to the proud, impatient and embittered leader that he is worthy of his place in the Company.

> "THERE IS ONE I COULD FOLLOW. THERE IS ONE I COULD CALL KING"

Thorin wears at his side the sword Orcrist, forged by the High Elves of the West, that he found in the trolls' cave. It is a powerful weapon with a fearsomely sharp, single-edged blade. Its hilt is formed from a single dragon's tooth, and indeed the runes that are inscribed into the blade spell out in the Elvish language of Sindarin the words NAGOL E-LYG or 'Tooth of-Snake [or dragon]'. But Orcs know it as the 'Goblin-cleaver'.

BALIN & DWALIN

Balin, being the elder statesman of the group, and regardless of his misgivings about the wisdom of their quest (since he has seen at first hand the horrors of the dragon and the desolation it has wrought) has shown himself to be a determined and effective fighter.

Like his brother Dwalin, and the leader of the Company, Balin is also a veteran of the Battle of Azanûlbizar, the great battle between the Dwarves and the Orcs, so he has seen death in conflict at first hand, and does not take it lightly.

Although he carries a sturdy weapon somewhere between a sword and an axe, which can both chop and stab, experience has taught him that even in a world populated with monstrous dragons, Wargs, Goblins and Orcs, a wise head and a cool tongue may prevail where an axe or sword are insufficient.

Moreover, Balin is not swayed by the temptations of the Dwarves' lost gold and gems, currently being greedily hoarded by Smaug.

His brother Dwalin, the professional soldier of the group, has had plenty of opportunity to show his mettle so far on the quest, having taken on hordes of Wargs, Orcs and Goblins, assailing them with his enormous battle-axes and warhammer. Even when he is disarmed, he uses the armoured vambraces on his forearms or the wicked knuckledusters on his hands!

He does not take much part in the songs and tales around the Company's campfires (his brother Balin does enough talking for the pair of them). He'd rather let his weapons do the talking, and so whenever he has a spare moment, he'll spend it sharpening and honing his blades.

Ever watchful and alert to the dangers that surround them, Dwalin awaits his chance to smash yet more Orc heads. Whilst defending his liege-lord and his fellows in the Company, he seizes every opportunity to take vengeance on those who have stolen and destroyed the heritage of his people.

KILI & FILI

Kili and Fili, the nephews of the leader of the Company, have come to the expedition with very little experience of battle, but the two young warrior princes are learning quickly. They have to, as dangers have been coming at them thick and fast!

Bristling with weapons – axes, swords, knives and bows – and with their sharp eyes and quick reflexes, they often find themselves posted on sentry-duty for the group. They were the first to spot that two of their ponies – Myrtle and Minty – had suddenly gone missing, captured by mountain trolls to eat for their supper. Even so, it was poor Bilbo Baggins they pushed forward to deal with the problem, rather than volunteering to take on the trolls themselves!

An expert with a bow, Kili has learned how to bring down a Warg with a single arrow, which is no mean feat, given the size and ferocity of these giant wild wolves. His reactions are so fast, he can even deflect shafts shot at him with the flat of his blade, and his brother Fili is equally swift and warlike.

It is important to them both to win fame and glory on this quest and to prove themselves worthy of accompanying their royal uncle, Thorin Oakenshield, of whom they are greatly in awe.

Reprimanded by Thorin for revelling with childish glee in tales of the bloodthirstiness of Orcs and Goblins, Kili and Fili now know for themselves what it is like to face these monsters in hand-to-hand combat. Now, they are rather less likely to joke about it.

But in times of ever-growing darkness and danger, Kili and Fili will be invaluable to the Company for far more than their fighting prowess and sharp eyes, possessed as they are of energy, optimism and good humour.

And being tall, for Dwarves, they are likely to catch the eye ... not only of the enemy, but of other folk of Middle-earth too.

OIN & GLOIN

Oin may be rather hard of hearing, particularly after having his beloved ear-trumpet trampled by evil Goblins in their caverns beneath the Misty Mountains, but he is just as fierce a warrior as any of his fellow Dwarves and shares their loathing of Goblins and Orcs and entrenched distrust of Elves.

He's more than happy to use his lethal iron staff, but the fearsome exterior of this Dwarf from the North hides a gentler soul than you might expect. Oin is not only an erudite and well-read scholar, he is also the Company's healer and a great expert in the identification and use of Middle-earth's plants. He carries with him a medical kit with which he can put together unguents and tisanes – healing salves and draughts. Indeed, it is sometimes said that the word 'ointment' derives from his name, so renowned is Oin for his herbal remedies. And there are bound to be occasions on the road ahead when such expert knowledge is urgently required.

Regaining their lost homeland holds a special meaning for Oin: apart from winning the kingdom of Erebor back for his cousin Thorin, Oin and his brother have a substantial sum of money invested in the venture!

His brother Gloin also has an interest in the material gains of the Company's quest. He is the coin-master and treasurer of the group, and always carries an abacus with him, along with his famous battle-axes.

Out of the entire Company, Gloin is the least diplomatic, the most likely to speak his mind and to lose his temper and start a fight. Luckily, his fighting skills are what benefit the Company most in these dark days. It seems appropriate that he should also be the group's fire-starter!

Fiery, too, is Gloin's braided red hair and beard. He shares his red hair with his young son Gimli, and his beautiful wife also sports a particularly fine beard. He carries portraits of both of them in a locket that he carries with him always.

There must be times on this quest – when surrounded by Goblins, Wargs and fierce Orcs, or taken prisoner by Elves or entering the dangerous territory of a dragon – when he is worried he will never see his family again.

DORI, NORI & ORI

Despite all the Company's travails, Dori manages to remain smart in his appearance, dapper, exact, maybe even a little prissy, with his hair and beard ever neatly braided. This care and precision is reflected in his wider character too, particularly when applied to his young brother Ori, whom he watches over like a mother hen. He is constantly ensuring that his younger sibling is safe and well, and eating his greens, even though Ori has a great aversion (like most Dwarves) to 'green food', and any meal that does not involve meat.

Being so aware of others all the time gives Dori a tendency towards anxiety and pessimism. It is easy for him to see the worst, and when that involves dangerous situations, that can be a bleak vision of the world indeed. But a determination to prevent the worst drives him to fight more fiercely than ever, to ensure his family and other members of the Company remain safe from harm.

Dori's other brother, Nori, came upon the quest partly as a means of getting his hands on some treasure, and any other booty that might come his way. This is partly because he may have fallen foul of the authorities (for Nori, despite coming from a good family has often strayed from the honest path and has a tendency to be a little light-fingered) and so has decided to make himself scarce. He is – typically of the Dwarven race – acquisitive, his motto being: 'what's mine is mine and what's yours is mine too'. It's the thought of all the gold and gems piled high in the halls of the lost kingdom of Erebor that drives his every step, rather than the wish to see Thorin reclaim his heritage. Nori has little respect for hierarchy or the re-establishment of a Dwarf-king, since no Dwarf-king has ever done anything for him!

But this greed does not make him a dislikeable character, quite the opposite in fact. Nori has a sharp eye and a ready smile, and he's a canny and practised fighter. He'll take on anyone who threatens his family or friends and will put his own life in danger without a second thought. He has no hesitation in taking on the monstrous Great Goblin beneath the Misty Mountains, and of all the Dwarves it was Nori who noticed that Bilbo had escaped when the rest of the Company were taken prisoner in Goblin Town. Those sharp eyes will be of great service as they venture into even more dangerous territory.

Dori and Nori are united in their concern for their little brother Ori, who is said to be the youngest member of the Company. It is possible that Fili and Kili are in fact younger than Ori; but their weapons training, cheeky confidence and general demeanour makes them seem older. Especially because Ori has been fussed over and coddled for much of his life, not only by his mother (whose knitted mittens and cosy hood he wears) but also by Dori. His youth manifests itself in his sweet and biddable manner, and through his interest in sketching and scribing, but it would be easy to underestimate this young Dwarf.

Beneath his mild exterior beats the heart of a would-be warrior, one who isn't afraid of anyone or anything. Even armed with only a little knife and a slingshot, Ori will without hesitation front up a ferocious Warg, and when he gets his hands on Dwalin's warhammer, any Orc who gets in his way had better watch out! Neither is he afraid of dragons (not that he has ever encountered one), and has vowed to give Smaug the Terrible a taste of Dwarvish iron "right up his jacksy!"

BIFUR, BOFUR & BOMBUR

Wounded in the battle to regain the Dwarf kingdom of Moria, which had been overrun by Orcs, Bifur is somewhat impaired by the remains of an axe left rusting in his skull. This injury had made him strangely inarticulate, able to communicate only by hand gestures and using the ancient Dwarvish language of Khuzdul, which only Gandalf is able to understand. The wound does not, however, stop him fighting valiantly against enemies. Already he has battled trolls, Goblins, Orcs and Wargs, and has remained unfazed.

Which is just as well, since there are far greater perils still to face as the Company make their way to the Lonely Mountain. There will be plenty more Orcs for Bifur to punish as he seeks the one who left the axe in him.

By contrast, his cousin Bofur is a talkative joker, an enthusiastic singer and musician. He is also wont to blurt out gleeful observations on the nature of dragons and the other dangers they face. But there is a lot more to him than the apparently simple miner that at first he seems, with his weighty mattock hefted on his shoulder. Bofur shares a remarkable rapport with Bilbo, seeing him as another outsider in the group, and he is surprisingly sympathetic to the hobbit when Bilbo shows doubts about staying with the Company.

Consistently optimistic, he's a very useful Dwarf to have around as the Company face ever greater dangers. Although his great love for ale may yet land him in more trouble than he'd like.

His brother Bombur is far too busy eating and preparing food to talk much, which is just as well, since Bofur more than makes up for him. But he looks up to his likeable brother and would follow him anywhere – over hill and dale, through hidden passes and over mountains, down rivers and into battle against unimaginable monsters. He may be naïve and gentle of soul, but he's also a rough and ready scrapper, more than happy to bash some Orcs over the head with his lethal ladle, or strangle a Goblin or two with the heavy looped braid of his red beard. He's even ready to take on a dragon, as long as there's a bit of gold to be had at the end of the day.

BILBO BAGGINS

As a youngster, Bilbo was always running off in search of Elves in the woods, staying out until after dark, and coming home covered in mud and twigs. But latterly he had become something of a stay-at-home hobbit, overly attached to his homely comforts – to his books and his armchair, to his warm hearth and full larder. He actively avoided adventures, exclaiming 'they make you late for dinner!'

But now he's a long way from home, and has had to get over his allergy to horsehair and dependence on such niceties as handkerchiefs. Now, he can never be that genteel, careful, comfortable hobbit again. Already on his journey away from Bag End he has experienced a great deal. He has seen, and even spoken with Elves. He has outwitted a trio of terrifying trolls. He has witnessed a battle between stone giants and journeyed high into the mountains and down below them. He has even fought against Orcs, Goblins and Wargs with his own sword – a real sword, no matter that Balin says it looks more like a letter-opener! And now he knows that the reality of the world is very different to the one he has come upon in his books and maps.

For Bilbo, more than any of the other members of Thorin's Company (apart, perhaps, from young Ori) this journey into the wilds will be a journey of discovery, not only of Middle-earth and the beauties and terrors it holds, but of himself. For that overly-cautious, old-before-his-time Bilbo Baggins, the hobbit who was too worried about his mother's lace doilies and fine dishes, is being transformed into a proper burglar. One possessed of ingenuity, sneakiness, courage and a remarkable sense of self-preservation.

> "I CAN'T JUST GO RUNNING OFF INTO THE BLUE! I AM A BAGGINS, OF BAG END."

But more than this, he has also discovered the importance of comradeship, of the need to depend on his friends and for them to depend on him. Repaying the debt to Thorin for saving his life when he fell from the mountain path above Imladris, Bilbo stood alone, protecting his leader's prone body from Azog the Defiler. In doing so, he has discovered within himself a hero he had never imagined existed.

The hero within Bilbo Baggins will be called upon many more times before this adventure is over.

THE CARROCK

Marking the boundary of Beorn's land is the great rock called the Carrock, a bald, jutting, natural rock formation which looks at some angles like a roaring bear's head. The Carrock rears straight up out of the ground like a final outcropping of the distant mountain range, right in the path of the Great River, which has been forced to run in a large meander around it.

Beorn has hewn a winding stairway into the living rock from the ground to the summit. The top of the Carrock offers sweeping views over the wide grassland plain and the great river Anduin that runs through it. From up there it is possible to see the eastern Misty Mountains, the whole of the Anduin Valley, right across Mirkwood Forest to the Lonely Mountain. It is thus a very useful lookout point for anyone interested in monitoring the comings and goings of travellers, or the evil that is creeping ever closer.

BEORN

Beorn, heavily muscled and nearly eight feet tall, with a great beard and mass of dark hair, is an imposing figure. Closer to a giant than a mere man, he is large enough to cast fear into Goblins and Orcs, let alone into such smaller beings as Dwarves and hobbits.

He lives in an oak-wood to the east of the Great River, in a large wooden house which lies behind a high thorn-hedge that is impossible to see through or scramble over. There he keeps cattle and horses that are nearly as big as he is, as well as dogs, sheep and chickens. He also keeps hives of great bees in pastures bursting with wildflowers. The drones are the size of small birds, with bands of gold on their furry black bodies that shine like fiery gold.

Like the wizard Radagast the Brown, Beorn loves the natural world and particularly his animals, and would never dream of eating any of his companions. Neither would he hunt any wild creatures, or do any of them harm. Instead, he makes bread, and eats it with cream from his cows and honey from his bees.

ONCE THERE WERE MANY LIKE ME, NOW THERE IS ONLY ONE.

He is the last of his people, but says that once there were many like him and that they were the first to live in the mountains before the Orcs came down from the north.

Orcs are extremely wary of straying near Beorn's domain, as well they might. For though Beorn escaped their cruel torture, he will never forget, or forgive. A Goblin's head is stuck on the gate outside his house, and a Warg-skin is nailed to a tree, as a warning to his enemies.

SKIN·CHANGERS

There are ancient tales of beings who are able to shape-shift, or to change their skins — men who can, under certain conditions, take on the form of wild animals like wolves or bears, in order to fight more fiercely or to harness a special and terrifying inner power they possess.

It is rumoured that Beorn is one such, and that when battle beckons or his temper is high he is able to transform himself from a huge muscular man into an enormous bear. Some say that he is a descendent of the first men. But others say he is descendant of the mountain bears, creatures so ancient they lived even before the giants came to Middle-earth, before the first men and the Goblins, before Smaug or the other fire-drakes were hatched.

Beorn does rather look like a bear even in his human-form. He loves honey, as many bears are known to do, and in one of the ancient languages his name is indeed the word for 'bear'. It is thought that as a bear he ranges far and wide and at night will often sit on the rocky island in the Great River Anduin known as the Carrock, watching the moon sink towards the Misty Mountains, growling in the tongue of bears.

MIRKWOOD

To the east of the Misty Mountains, across the Great River Anduin, lies the huge forest of Mirkwood, once known as Greenwood the Great. A once beautiful forest, its pathways were lit by the sun and swept by soft winds. But a sickness has fallen upon the Greenwood and it has become a wild, dark place into which the sun rarely shines. The trees in Mirkwood have become gnarled and tangled, their branches twisted and weighed down by trailing ivy and lichen. The roots of the forest trees sprawl and crawl across the forest floor, always ready to catch an unwary foot, and among them blind, pale creatures slither silently. The deep green gloom is broken only by the fall of faint white spores. All manner of poisonous fungi sprout amongst the fallen deadwood, and unknown herbs with a rank, unpleasant smell grow here now.

Ruled by the King of the Wood-elves, the forest's wide, sunlit roads were once traversed by merchants and travellers from every quarter of Middle-earth, but now no safe paths exist through the forest. Even the old Elf-path which runs from the Forest Gate to the Elven king's halls, which Thorin travelled so often in his youth, is now fraught with danger.

The only safe road to the Long Lake and the Lonely Mountain skirts the forest to the north, over the Edge of the Wild, and it is two hundred miles longer than the direct route. To the south lies the lair of the Necromancer, and so, overlooked by his dark tower, Thorin and his Company must take their chances with the forest path.

Nasty, dense cobwebs thread between the trees and strange black squirrels dart and scuttle. The air is unmoving, stuffy and hard to breathe. Even Dwarves, used to dark tunnels underground, would feel claustrophobic in such a place; and at night it is even worse, for there is a sense of eyes staring out of the trees, pale, bulbous eyes, and unseen things rustle in the undergrowth. Thousands of grey and black moths, some as big as a hand, flutter through the gloom, and huge bats flap and chitter in the night air.

Gandalf, who knows the forest well, has warned the Company not to stray from the path, for there are enchanted circles of light and a deep black stream that if stepped into traps incautious travellers and lures them into a dangerous, dreamy state in which they will be easy prey for the creatures of the wood.

SPIDERS

It was Radagast the Brown who witnessed giant black spiders making their way out of the abandoned fort of Dol Guldur into the forest of Mirkwood. Spawned by an ancient monster, now they have become a multitude, and ever more bold in their wanderings. Lately, they have even encroached as far west as Radagast's home of Rhosgobel, such is their daring and their confidence in the growing tide of evil that is creeping ever westwards.

The spiders are fat-bodied and monstrous, as big as a man, with great hairy legs and wicked nippers with which they use to sting and numb their prey.

The huge webs they spin shroud the trees and festoon their branches. The threads of these webs are unnaturally strong and sticky, and once caught in them, it is very hard to escape. As soon as prey is caught, the spiders sense the vibrations in the threads and immediately scuttle to wrap their prisoner into bundles from which they cannot extricate themselves. These cocoons hang like ripe fruit from the branches of the trees to act as the spiders' larder from which they can draw off the rich juice of their prey to feed upon as the fancy takes them.

DOL GULDUR

In a remote south-western part of the great forest of Mirkwood, upon a high point known as the Hill of Sorcery, there lies a forbidding ruin, known in the language of the Elves as Dol Guldur.

Once, the Elves of the Woodland Realm frequented this region, but growing tensions with the Elves of Lórien in the west persuaded them to abandon the fortress and it had long fallen into disuse. Now, its forked and blasted stones rear up in broken towers, below which lie dungeons and torture chambers. And at its centre, a courtyard containing nine niches, each capped by a triangular portico.

Nine. A powerful number in the history of Middle-earth: nine Rings of Power were given to nine kings of Men by the Dark Lord, Sauron. And very soon those kings lost their humanity to the power of the Rings and the lord who ruled them, becoming wraith-like, ravening spirits bent on evil purposes. Ringwraiths, Men deemed them then, or Nazgûl as the Dark Lord called them.

The greatest of these kings was the Witch-king of Angmar. By some curious coincidence, Radagast the Brown came to find the Witch-king's sword in Dol Guldur, even though the morgul-blade had long ago been buried with him. The blade was shut inside a rock-tomb far away, and his tomb was sealed shut by a powerful spell, never to be opened. Radagast passed this blade to Gandalf, who showed it to Saruman and the Lady Galadriel at the meeting of the White Council in Rivendell as evidence that dark powers were gathering at Dol Guldur.

"ALWAYS YOU MUST MEDDLE, LOOKING FOR TROUBLE WHERE NONE EXISTS"

But when Gandalf puts such questions to the highest of the wizards Saruman the White, he waves them away as fanciful, and accuses Gandalf and Radagast of looking for trouble where there is none. But the Grey wizard and the Brown wizard have been watching the signs of rising evil for too long to ignore them.

Something has taken over the abandoned fortress at Dol Guldur, something wicked. Something terrifying. Something that attracts other evil things to it ... Orcs, Wargs and giant spiders ... and maybe Ringwraiths too.

It is whispered that this being is one known as the Necromancer.

THE NECROMANCER

There is once more an occupant in the eerie abandoned fortress of Dol Guldur. Some strange, uncanny power has established its stronghold in this most remote and unwelcoming of ruins. None have yet seen it, but its effects are being felt far and wide.

The shadow of fear and a sickness born of dark magic is seeping out from Dol Guldur. Stretching across Mirkwood and beyond, it poisons all in its path: laying waste the beauty of the ancient Greenwood, corrupting its flora and fauna, darkening its once wide and sunlit paths. It is rumoured that at the root of this dark power lies a being known only as the Necromancer.

When confronted by Gandalf's suspicions that the being occupying the Hill of Sorcery, though formless and faceless, is the shadow of an ancient horror, capable of summoning the spirits of the dead, Saruman dismisses the idea as absurd, claiming that the Necromancer is no more than a mere human conjuror dabbling with black magic.

But there is evidence to the contrary, the morgul-blade, for one, and can it be sheer coincidence that whatever dark power has made its home here should have chosen a ruin that lies so close to the Gladden Fields, where the River Gladden joins the Great River Anduin?

For it was at that junction where the One Ring – the master ring forged to control all the other rings of power – was lost in a bygone age. It had been cut from the hand of the Dark Lord Sauron when he was defeated in the last great battle in Middle-earth by Isildur, King of Men. But when Isildur was pursued and ambushed by Orcs, he was killed and the Ring was lost in that river.

Where it was found, many years later by a certain creature known as Gollum. It is the very ring that Bilbo now unwittingly carries in his pocket, the one he found in Gollum's lair beneath the Misty Mountains, and won by unfair means in their riddle-contest.

There are too many coincidences here for Gandalf's liking. Watching and spying will have to be taken one step further. He will have to visit the Hill of Sorcery for himself if the true identity of the Necromancer is to be revealed.

Azog the Defiler

Long ago, at the Battle of Azanulbizar, the Orcs of the Misty Mountains fought against an army of Dwarves outside the east gate of Moria. The Dwarves were victorious, but at a terrible cost. Many brave Dwarves were lost in that battle, including the king himself, Thrór, father of Thráin, and grandfather of Thorin Oakenshield. It was the White Orc of Gundabad, Azog the Defiler who took Thrór's life, and indeed his head.

But Thrór's grandson, maddened with grief and fury, set upon the Pale Orc to avenge his king's death. With his giant mace, Azog disarmed the young Dwarf prince, and as he raised his weapon to smash his skull, Thorin picked up an oaken branch lying on the ground and used it as a shield. As Azog swung his mace again, Thorin, grabbing a sword lying nearby, managed to cut off the Orc's mace-arm, just below the elbow; and at last the Dwarves won the day.

Thorin has always believed that Azog died of the wound, but he did not. Now wearing a cruel prosthetic arm fashioned from spiked metal, he rides a giant white Warg. At his belt he wears the

"I WANT THE HEAD OF THE DWARF!"

skull of slain King Thrór. Having sworn to wipe out the line of Durin, he intends to add the skull of Thorin Oakenshield to his collection of battle-trophies. Now he and his pack of Orcs hunt Thorin and his Company, to the death. Already, they have pursued them across the Wilds, over heath and hill, even up into the trees from which they were fortuitously rescued by the Eagles.

He will surely learn that the line of Durin will not be so easily broken.

Dwarves & Elves:
A History of Enmity

Elves have no love for Dwarves, and Dwarves none for Elves. In bygone ages there have even been wars between the two, stemming from greed and misunderstanding, from small grievances that were allowed to brew over the years into deep suspicion and hatred.

And so when the dragon fell upon the kingdom of Erebor and the Dwarves were in the greatest peril, the King of the Woodland Realm refused to help. Astride his great elk, King Thranduil ignored their cries for aid and turned away, unwilling to risk the lives of any of his Elves against the terror of the fire-drake.

Maybe, if the Wood-elves had joined the Dwarves in opposition to the dragon, together they might have defeated the fire-breathing monster, although many would surely have died in the attempt. It is, perhaps, understandable that Thranduil considered the risk as too great; but Dwarves are a proud and stubborn folk and perceived this turning away as a deadly insult.

Losing so many of their folk and their kingdom under the Mountain was bad enough, but worse was to follow. For in the wake of this catastrophe, the Elves did nothing to help those Dwarves who survived, not even to aid them in rooting out the Orcs

who swarmed into the caverns of Moria. Instead, they were left to wander in the wilderness, a once-mighty people brought low, Prince Thorin taking work wherever he could find it, often blacksmithing in the villages of Men, while his subjects scratched a living as tinkers and toy-makers, miners and smiths.

But the memory of all he had seen in that fateful time was burned into Thorin's mind; the mountain on fire, the dragon invading the ancient halls, the loss of their close-guarded treasure, the deaths of so many of his people, and what he saw as the callous indifference of the Elves, and their betrayal of his father and grandfather. He would never forgive, and never forget.

And for their part, the Elves are little better, refusing to recognize that the Dwarves may have cause for their grudge, instead regarding them as embittered, graceless, and greedy for treasure. It is a great tragedy that these two proud peoples should be so at odds.

THE ELVES OF THE WOODLAND REALM

The Elves are the Firstborn of Middle-earth, having been awakened by Illúvatar long before any other race. As a result, they have a special relationship with the natural world, one that requires they be watchful guardians. This relationship is enhanced by the essential immortality of the Elves, since they succumb neither to sickness or old age but only to violence, enabling them to take a very long view of events, and to guard the memories and history of the world. It may be a full century before an Elf comes to maturity and to their full growth and understanding; in addition, they have few offspring, so each Elf-child is nurtured and valued deeply.

Which may in part explain why King Thranduil of the Wood-elves was reluctant to involve his people in the defence of the Dwarves and their realm. With so long to live and so much to know and to experience, for an Elf to give his or her life for another's cause represents an unmatchable sacrifice.

There are different branches of Elven kindred. Those who dwell in the forested regions of Middle-earth are known generally as Silvan Elves. They have come to live mainly near the Misty Mountains – either in Lórien, under the care of Lord Celeborn and the Lady Galadriel (and this group is known as the Galadhrim); or in the north of what used to be the Greenwood and is now called Mirkwood, under the rule of King Thranduil. These are the Elves of the Woodland Realm, or the Wood-elves.

All Elves represent the true spirit of Middle-earth. They are graceful, beautiful, powerful and swift. The Elves of Rivendell are tall and elegant, as befits their beautiful refuge. The Galadhrim have pale hair, and wear gold and silver robes that echo the light-filled groves, and their stature mimics the towering pale mallorn trees of the realm of Lórien. Meanwhile, the Wood-elves tend to be a little shorter and more rooted to the earth, their choice of colours more earthy – russets and ochre, bone and browns – to echo the denser, shade-filled forest of Mirkwood.

KING THRANDUIL

The king of the Wood-elves is Thranduil, a stern, severe, imposing Elf with pale skin and long, silver-blond hair. He wears a crown wound about with red leaves and berries in autumn, to mirror the season in his realm; and in spring a coronet worked with woodland flowers. In his hand he bears a staff of oak, symbolizing his sovereignty over the Woodland Realm. His sigil is the great elk, giant antlers adorn his throne and are worked into the silver of his crown and the motif of his robes.

King Thranduil has a weakness for precious metals and gems but also an innate desire to reclaim what is rightfully his. His overwhelming need for justice has created the rift between the Elves and the Dwarves. Because the Elves do not work metal, Thranduil made a bargain with the Dwarves of Erebor, under Thorin's grandfather, Thrór, to shape his raw gold, silver, and white and silver gems into wondrous jewellery. The Elves claim that the Dwarves were so overcome by avarice at the sight of such treasure that they stole it. But the Dwarves tell another story: that Thrór took only what was due to them because Thranduil refused to pay them the agreed price, and so they kept the jewels as recompense.

Whichever side of the tale is true, what cannot be denied is that in the Dwarves' hour of need, when the dragon Smaug stormed their mountain kingdom with fire and fury, King Thranduil ignored the call for help. The Dwarves of Erebor were destroyed, burned to death in the caves and tunnels of their mountain. Enmity and distrust has lain between the two peoples ever since that time and the wound of this betrayal sits deep in the heart of the Dwarves' king-in-exile, Thorin Oakenshield.

Indeed, a great and general distrust has entered the Woodland Realm, borne on the tide of creeping evil that infuses Mirkwood Forest. As it has become darker and more poisoned, so have the minds of the Elves of the wood become ever more insular and closed. Elves are generally distrustful of Dwarves, but the Wood-elves harbour a greater distrust than any other of their kind. This is partly because of the historical enmity between the two peoples, but also because of their close trading relationship with the Men of Dale and the Long Lake, who blame the Dwarves for attracting the dragon to their region by amassing so much treasure. Now Thranduil's realm exists in a militarized state, ever wary, ever defensive, ready to close themselves off from the rest of the world and let the other peoples of Middle-earth fend for themselves.

THE ELVENKING'S PALACE

The palace of the King of the Woodland Realm lies on the eastern edge of Mirkwood, above a fast-running river, which flows into the Long Lake below the Lonely Mountain. Here there lies a town of Men with whom the Elves still trade.

His palace consists of a series of caverns which lie concealed behind a pair of huge stone doors accessible only via an ornate wooden bridge over a precipitous ravine. Within the doors are to be found vast, elegant halls, winding passages and many chambers which lie entwined among the roots of the giant trees that grow above it. Thranduil's throne room is hewn into the living rock, vast tree-roots making a pattern of natural sculptures down the walls.

Most of the Wood-elves live in the woods, as is their heritage and habit. However, the palace serves not only as a royal residence but also as a fortress against their enemies, a dungeon for their prisoners and as the king's stronghold; for he has a great deal of treasure to safeguard.

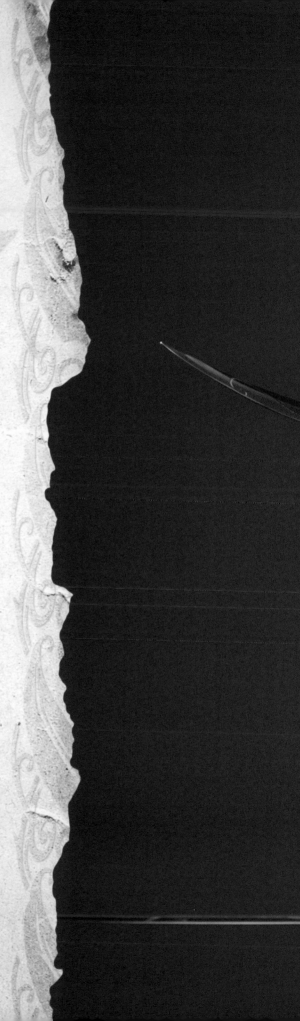

LEGOLAS

The son of King Thranduil of the Wood-elves is Prince Legolas, whose name in Elvish means 'Greenleaf'. He is indeed as tall, strong and graceful as a young tree of the Woodland Realm. Lithe and fast, he can run swiftly and silently and is possessed of the extraordinary vitality of his kind. He has his father's clear-cut features and pale-gold hair, his piercing eyes and keen intellect. But where Thranduil has become suspicious of strangers to the point of outright hostility, closed, stern and brooding, Legolas has the honest curiosity and open mind of the young idealist.

He is one of the Woodland Realm's greatest warriors, fast, powerful and tireless. His great speed, strong arm and sharp eyes make him an expert with a war-bow. He also wields two elf-knives, long and white with filigreed blades, which in his hands are the most deadly weapons an Orc is likely to face.

As an implacable foe to his enemies, he is thus a formidable protector of his people, in particular his fellow warrior, Tauriel. Should any approach her with ill-intent, be they Orc or Dwarf, they do so at their peril.

TAURIEL

The head of the Silvan guard is a young Elf called Tauriel, but do not be fooled by her youth or her apparently fragile beauty, for she is a formidable warrior with both bow and arrow and the beautiful but deadly filigreed daggers she carries wherever she goes. In the tough, military culture that has come to characterize the Woodland Realm, she must be a truly extraordinary fighter to have been appointed to such an elevated and crucial position at so tender an age (for she is barely six hundred years old: hardly more than a child by Elven standards).

Tauriel has been raised in the Woodland Realm at Thranduil's court ever since her parents were murdered by Orcs. Thranduil looks upon her almost as a daughter and Legolas has been her friend since her childhood. In her eyes Legolas is like a brother.

And yet despite her lethal killing skills, her warlike aspect and her highly responsible position, Tauriel has a passionate, playful and adventurous − maybe even slightly rebellious − spirit. It may be that she does not view the race of Dwarves as enemies, especially if they are taller or fairer than most of their kind.

She also has a yearning for a world in which Elves do not close themselves away in dark caves and fortresses and shut their gates against the rest of the world. Instead, Tauriel yearns to go out into the wilds, to combat the evil that is encroaching upon their realm and to meet it head to head and hand to hand. And if that means avenging the deaths of her parents on the monstrous Orcs that murdered them, so much the better.

The lakeside town of Esgaroth, now known by Men simply as Lake-town, used to be the greatest centre of trade in all of northern Middle-earth. Fleets of boats plied their trade across the Long Lake and anchored in its harbour, and merchants – from the races of Men, Elves and Dwarves – came from far and wide to do business in its marketplace.

Cargoes of gold and silks, jewels and fine mithril mail were traded here, and riches flowed down into the town from the Halls of Erebor. But with the fall of the Dwarven kingdom, those days are long gone and now Lake-town is little more than a forgotten outpost. It remains as a ramshackle collection of wharves, bridges and creaking walkways, where wooden piles and the abandoned carcasses of old boats, broken barrels and mouldy sacks rot down into the stinking mud.

The houses were once smart and fine, brightly painted and adorned with hand-carvings and pretty shutters, the pride and joy of the families who owned them. The canals were alive with little pleasure craft and fishermen landed their shining catches on neatly ordered quays. The marketplace was heaving with healthy livestock, colourful market-stalls and throngs of traders and happy customers. But now the houses are foundering so that all are askew, the thatch is full of vermin, and no one has had the will or the means to repaint them. The canals are full of refuse, flies and stench and the long wooden bridge which is the town's only connection to land is in disrepair. The streets are full of beggars and ragged children, disease and despair are rife and there is noise, filth, disorder and confusion wherever you look.

"ONCE, WE WERE LORDS OF THESE LANDS."

Worse than this: red tape abounds. There are tollgates where once the ways were free for all to travel and every activity is bound by statutes and bureaucracy. It seems you need a licence to do anything in Lake-town, and licences cost money. But where does the money go? Not into the town's coffers to improve the place for everyone, or to provide for the sick and needy. Oh no. The authorities are lining their pockets with bribes, and the man at the top – as is always the way when corruption is rife – is profiting most of all.

THE MASTER OF LAKE-TOWN

Men generally rise to positions of power usually for one of two reasons – because they have a burning desire to see justice done and the people governed with fairness and competence; or because they hanker for the opportunities such an elevated position will afford them in lining their own pockets and increasing their personal status and influence. The Master of Lake-town is, unfortunately, one of the latter, a deeply venal, sly and conniving politician who has risen to the position of Master through manifold acts of corruption and the manipulation of those less cunning or determined than himself.

The perpetuation of the system requires that all are either invested in it and therefore see no profit in upsetting the status quo, or are so oppressed that they are unable to mount a challenge to it. This is how the Master runs Lake-town, and thus how he maintains his position.

The Master loves gold and riches almost as much as any dragon. No one is capable of loving gold more than a dragon – not a man, nor a hobbit nor even a prince of Dwarves – for dragons are vast, elemental beings whose very nature is bound up with the fire of gold. But the Master of Lake-town is a close second. He revels not in the beauty of the yellow metal itself, but in the glories of wealth which when bartered with, gold may provide him with.

HIS PRIVATE SECRETARY IS ALFRID, A DEEPLY OFFICIOUS AND CONNIVING MAN, AND THUS THE PERFECT SERVANT FOR SUCH A CORRUPT AND SCHEMING POLITICIAN.

The finest luxuries adorn his home, the most expensive wines are in his cellar, the richest foods in his larder and the heaviest brocades are on his capacious frame. But as the old saying goes, you can't buy taste, and the Master is a slovenly man, gross and greedy in his appetites, so lacking in personal hygiene as to be the very opposite of fastidious. Filth adorns his robes, old food his moustache and beard; and the rank smell of cowardice follows him wherever he goes.

BARD THE BARGEMAN

It is hard to be an upstanding citizen under the repressive regime in Lake-town, but there is at least one honest, decent, hard-working man amidst all the corruption, fear and poverty.

Bard is a bargeman by trade, spending long, cold days bringing back the barrels that have floated down to Lake-town from Mirkwood and the Woodland Realm. The Elves of the Woodland Realm exchange goods with the men of Lake-town via these barrels, sending the empties back into the river that flows beneath the cellars of the Elvenking's palace down to the Long Lake. It is Bard's job to hook the barrels out of the water, haul them aboard the barge, and make the load safe. It's hard, exhausting, freezing work, but he does it with a will to provide for his family. And if he has a chance to land a few fish for the table, or to sell at the quays, so much the better.

Such menial work is a long way from his heritage, as a scion of one of the noblest families of Dale, the city that was destroyed by the dragon Smaug, from which the few survivors fled with only the clothes on their backs. The refugees who made it to Lake-town nearly two hundred years ago fell on very hard times indeed. Regarded as outsiders, even as outcasts, they have never been

made to feel welcome, and as a descendant of these exiled people, Bard is no exception.

It is perhaps one reason that his family is so important to him: he has forged a strong, tight-knit family, one which relies on no one else. For Lake-town is filled with spies and tattle-tales who snoop for the Master and his minions, where you have the sense of being watched all the time, and can be imprisoned on the smallest of trumped-up accusations. It is dangerous to trust anyone, especially if you're already seen as a troublemaker who speaks unpopular truth. Everything Bard does is for the good of his three children: his eldest, Sigrid, his fast-growing son, Bain, and his youngest daughter, Tilda. Since their mother died in childbirth, Bard has had to be both mother and father to the children and although he may appear inscrutable, stern and dark of countenance to the outside world, to his children he is a hero and they love him dearly.

Bain in particular idolizes his tough, practical, courageous father. With a boy's natural love of ancient tales of legend and deeds of derring-do, and his fascination with weapons, he sees his father as a hero. And when someone looks up to you with such unwavering belief, it's impossible not to try to live up to their expectation.

DURIN'S DAY & MOON RUNES

The map that guides the Company was made by the Dwarf-king Thror, who gave it to his son Thráin for safekeeping. Athough it was long thought lost, Gandalf managed to restore the map to the line of Durin, passing it to Thráin's only heir, Thorin Oakenshield. It shows a plan of the Lonely Mountain, site of the lost Dwarven kingdom of Erebor, with the dragon marked upon it in red. Not that you need to mark a dragon in red on a map in order to find it in real life ...

According to the runes inscribed on the map, beneath a hand pointing to the west side of the mountain, there is a secret entrance into Erebor, the door to a passage leading to the Lower Halls. Those runes, which read, 'Five feet high the door and three may walk abreast', suggest that this entrance would be too small for a dragon to pass through, especially one that has incinerated a large number of the Dwarves of Erebor and the Men of Dale.

And with the map comes a pewter key with a long barrel and intricate wards; a key that was also passed to Gandalf by Thráin for safekeeping.

But how to find the door? It is well known that when Dwarves fashion a hidden door it stays hidden, completely invisible to the eye, appearing exactly like the surrounding rock from which it is carved. And on a hillside as large as the west slopes of the Lonely Mountain, that is a lot of rock indeed, particularly when there is the briefest space of time in which to find the keyhole.

At Rivendell, Gandalf the Grey asked Lord Elrond to examine the map for the Company in case it concealed any further clues, despite the distrust of the Dwarves. Lucky that he did! For as the moonlight fell upon the map, Elrond discovered the existence of 'cirth ithil', Elvish for 'moon runes'.

Moon runes, invented by ancient Dwarves and written by them with silver pens, can be read only by the light of a moon with the same shape and season as the day on which they were written. The moon runes on Thorin's map were written on a midsummer's eve by the light of a crescent moon nearly two hundred years ago. With immense good fortune, the same moon shone the night the Company arrived in Rivendell.

If held up to this very particular light, this is what the moon-runes say: 'Stand by the grey stone when the thrush knocks and the setting sun with the last of Durin's Day will shine upon the keyhole.' Durin was Thorin's ancestor, father of the fathers of the eldest race of Dwarves, the Longbeards, and Durin's Day represents their New Year, the first day of the last moon of autumn. Dwarves still call it Durin's Day when the last moon of autumn and the sun are in the sky together.

But summer is passing fast and that fateful day will soon be upon them ...

THE PROPHECY

The King beneath the Mountain
The King of carven stone
The lord of silver fountains
Shall come into his own.

His crown shall be upholden
His harp shall be restrung
The halls shall echo golden
To songs of yore resung.

The woods shall wave on mountains,
And grass beneath the sun
His wealth shall flow in fountains
And the rivers golden run

The bells shall run in gladness,
At the Mountain-king's return
And all shall fail in sadness
And the lake shall shine and burn.

DRAGONS

Never underestimate the malice of a dragon. They are cunning beyond measure and dreadfully cruel of heart.

In Hobbiton, dragons are only things of make-believe, to be conjured by wizards' fireworks, no more frightening than fairy dust. But there is a long history of very real, very terrifying dragons in Middle-earth and they have existed since the earliest times and are recorded in the annals of the wars of the First Age.

There are various types of dragons: the cold-drakes, who have no fire in them; the fire-drakes, who fly and can issue great gouts of flame; and some vast dragons that lumber on four legs and breathe fire, but are flightless. Such a one was Glaurung, bred long, long ago by the Dark Lord Morgoth to be used as a terrifying weapon in the Siege of Angband. During this siege, thousands of Elves were killed and incinerated (another reason, no doubt, why King Thranduil is wary of tangling with dragons). Glaurung then went on to lead an army of Orcs, proving himself a cunning and ruthless commander.

And there was Ancalagon the Black, often said to be the mightiest of all, who led a host of

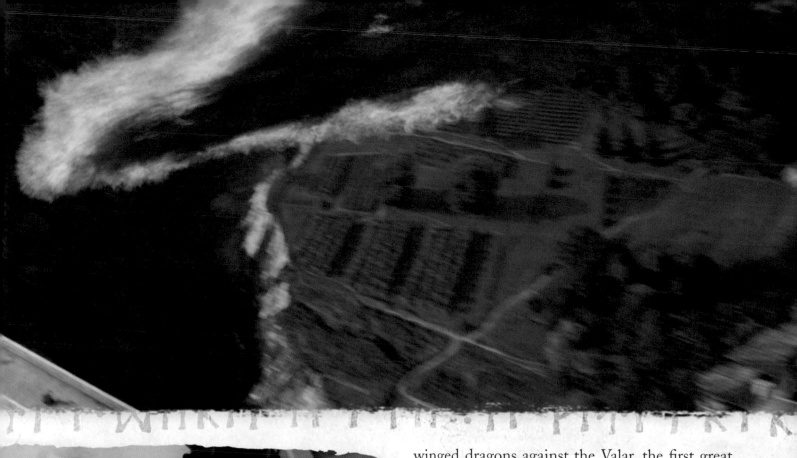

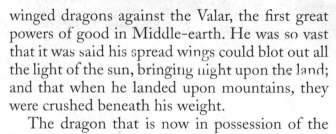

winged dragons against the Valar, the first great powers of good in Middle-earth. He was so vast that it was said his spread wings could blot out all the light of the sun, bringing night upon the land; and that when he landed upon mountains, they were crushed beneath his weight.

The dragon that is now in possession of the Lonely Mountain is an immense fire-drake from the north named Smaug. Having incinerated the city of Dale, he thereby rid himself of the annoying Dwarves who once inhabited the kingdom of Erebor – the only thing that had stood between him and the immense hoard of gold and gems that lay within the mountain. For now, Smaug is only interested in being left in peace to revel in his treasure, for all dragons love gold with a fierce, unquenchable desire.

A tense, hard-won peace has lain over Middle-earth for four hundred years: but Gandalf and Radagast are convinced that dark powers are rising once more. Orcs and Wargs abound, the Greenwood has been poisoned by evil, beings long thought buried appear to have risen. If this is so, what would happen if this massive, city-destroying dragon were to be persuaded there was yet more treasure to be amassed by joining forces with those dark powers? Such a catastrophe is simply unimaginable ...

THE
DESOLATION
OF SMAUG

ONCE THESE SLOPES WERE LINED WITH
WOODLANDS AND THE TREES WERE
FILLED WITH BIRDSONG

On the map Thorin Oakenshield carries with him there is inscribed this forbidding legend: 'The Desolation of Smaug'.

To the south and west of the Lonely Mountain (for you must turn the map on its side to align it in the usual way, with north and south) lies a great swathe of land which is blackened and burned, where nothing lives any more except for a pale, etiolated, sickly regrowth. Once there had been greenwoods full of leaf here, where woodland creatures made their burrows and birds their nests. There were water meadows filled with flowers and sheltered valleys vibrant with moss. The hillsides were bright with heather and bracken and bilberry. But now the riverbanks are bare and rocky, the cliffs grey and silent. Of the woods nothing remains but the charred stumps of trees. And nothing now moves through this scene of desolation except for the occasional grim black crow.

But worst of all is the ruined city of Dale, which lies right before the gigantic gates into the mountain kingdom of Erebor. Once this had been a thriving city of Men, full of elegant bell-towers, domes and cupolas, wide marketplaces and thoroughfares. Their houses were of warm ochre stone, roofs tiled with terracotta, balconies adorned with pots of flowers and their courtyard gardens abundant with vines and fruit trees. But now there are just grey ruins. Tumbles of stone, piles of charred timber, thousands of corpses frozen in time, like the victims of volcanoes.

SUCH WANTON DEATH WAS DEALT
THAT DAY, FOR THIS CITY OF MEN
WAS NOTHING TO SMAUG

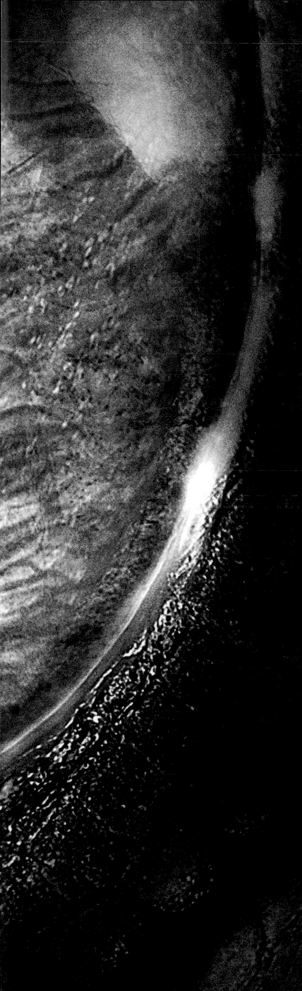

SMAUG THE MAGNIFICENT

There is nothing a dragon covets more than gold. The desire to amass treasure, to surround himself with it, to gloat over it, to count it, to feel it rub against his scales. This desire is as fierce as the love of life to a dragon.

It is gold that drew Smaug to the Lonely Mountain all the way from the Withered Heath far to the north. For the Dwarves of Erebor had collected a tremendous hoard of gold and gems inside their kingdom. Seams of precious of diamonds, rubies and sapphires ran like rivers through the rock there, to be mined by the Dwarves in vast quarries that they excavated out of the heart of the mountain.

Dragons have an acute sense of smell. They can even smell gold — and Smaug is no exception. Drawn by the treasure-hoard he coveted, he would not rest until he had destroyed the Men and Dwarves who came between him and his desire. He unleashed torrents of fire upon any foolish enough to stand in his way, on the slow, the young, the sick and the unlucky.

Now he lies in the treasure-halls of Erebor, far down in mountain's roots, soaking up the reflected glory of the hoard he has stolen from the Dwarves and regards as his own. It encrusts his scales, making for him a second glittering skin of armour. To immerse himself in gold and jewels, to sleep on a vast bed of treasure: only this makes any dragon content and he will guard his plunder as long as he lives. Which is usually a very, very long time.

The best advice is always to avoid a dragon, and to give them as wide a berth as you can possibly manage. For as well as dealing death with fire and claw, they are sly and cunning and possessed of strange magic. To engage a dragon in any sort of conversation is extremely perilous, for they will trap you with your own words. And woe betide you if you should happen to look into one of their vast, gleaming eyes — as brilliant and faceted as any jewel. If you ever find yourself in such a perilous situation, remember that the only way you may survive is to talk flatteringly to them, for dragons are immensely vain.

First U.S. edition

First published by HarperCollins*Publishers* 2013

Text copyright © Jude Fisher 2013
Foreword copyright © Richard Armitage 2013

The Hobbit: The Desolation of Smaug Visual Companion is a
companion to the film *The Hobbit: The Desolation of Smaug*
and is published with the permission, but not the approval,
of the Estate of the late J.R.R. Tolkien.

The Hobbit is published in the United States by
Houghton Mifflin Harcourt.

For information about permission to reproduce selections
from this book, write to Permissions, Houghton Mifflin
Harcourt Publishing Company, 215 Park Avenue South,
New York, New York 10003.

Library of Congress Cataloging-in-Publication Data
is available.
ISBN 978-0-547-89874-2

Printed and bound in Spain
HC 10 9 8 7 6 5 4 3 2 1

Acknowledgements
Thanks are due to many people in the making of this
Visual Companion, among them my agent Jonathan
Lloyd, publisher David Brawn and editor Natasha Hughes,
designer Ben Gardiner, cover designer Stuart Bache, Charles
Light and Kathy Turtle for production, Eleanor Goymer,
Elena Thompson and Caroline Crofts in the rights team,
and Ann Bissell in publicity. At Warner Bros., I must thank
Victoria Selover, Melanie Swartz, Elaine Piechowski,
Susannah Scott, and Jill Benscoter and Jayne Trotman; in
New Zealand Judy Alley, Melissa Booth and Ceris Price,
Alan Lee, John Howe, Chris and Dan Hennah, and Matt
Dravitzki; Richard Taylor, Ann Maskrey, Peter Swords-King
and most importantly Peter Jackson and the filmmakers,
cast, crew and fellow author Brian Sibley for invaluable
insights into the characters and world of *The Hobbit*.